Maria Weston Chapman

Memorial of Harriet Martineau

Maria Weston Chapman

Memorial of Harriet Martineau

ISBN/EAN: 9783337120733

Printed in Europe, USA, Canada, Australia, Japan

Cover: Foto ©Raphael Reischuk / pixelio.de

More available books at **www.hansebooks.com**

Memorials

of

Harriet Martineau.

Foreign Life.

" He that would bring back the wealth of the
Indies must carry out the wealth of the Indies: — and
the knowledge of this, was what caused the unusual
excitement in the public mind of America when it
became known that Harriet Martineau was about
to visit the United States. They had been annoyed
by incompetent persons, assuming to be their factors &
interpreters to Europe; but here was one of a different
type; & the first thought was of the return freight-
age.

No English traveller had before visited the country
with so brilliant a prestige. She brought out such
a reputation for learning as well as genius, — for pi-
ety as well as power, — for trained critical ability, as
well as natural observing faculty, — for thorough

. . . . . succeed to this leadership in their turn, longed to express their grateful acknowledgments of the pleasant

knowledge of England as well as kindly dispositions towards America, that the statesman-like acquirements & literary success which had constituted her greatness at home, were but few among many of the considerations that made her fame abroad.

She came with a social prestige to the showy dwellers of Atlantic cities, who had read in the London newspapers that the services of the police were needed to keep order in the line of carriages at her soirées. These were the persons whose ambition, or rather lack of genuine self-esteem was shown in America by their efforts, — in humble imitation of the obnoxious class distinctions which the best Englishmen thought the least worth perpetuating, — to keep up among themselves dim traditional notions & literary illusions unrecognized by the law at large. Her aristocratic friendships were more in their minds than her Democratic sympathies; & they loved the reflected light of such glories.

She came, too, with an unequalled religious prestige to her own denomination, which, unlike Unitarianism in England, was here at that time, an influential one for its wealth, social position & literary culture; — and she came with unprecedented claims on the minds of leaders in National & State politics; — while our "Millions," — the reading public, who were all hoping to succeed to this leadership in their turn, longed to express their grateful acknowledgments of the pleasant

awakening she had given to their moral sense.

For what had principally marked the time immediately preceding her arrival, forty years ago, was a singular moral apathy or paralysis, which made its literature, politics & religion all seem either formal & unreal, or disproportionate & extravagant: — the smooth, relenting movement of the state engine, with great noise & bustle among the conductors. Life was fast degenerating into insipid sentimentalism or ridiculous caricature, among all who were not actually struggling for a living. There was no advance; for that part of the nation that ought, by position & cultivated intelligence to have led, had lost the way.

But, popularly accepted & borne onward by the admiration of all, Harriet Martineau enjoyed unequalled opportunities for coming to just conclusions about America. She landed in New York in the middle of September, 1834, & travelled first in the States of New York, New Jersey, Massachusetts & Pennsylvania, examining their cities, villages & manufactures, visiting friends & making pilgrimages to every scene of moral interest or natural sublimity & beauty. She remained six weeks in Philadelphia, where there are as many circles of society, as at Geneva, each personally unknown to the other, in constant intercourse with many of them. She remained three weeks in Baltimore, the Capital of the Slave-State of Maryland, before

establishing herself at Washington for the session of Congress. While in this capital of the nation she was earnestly sought by all the eminent men of all parties, among senators, representatives, judges of the Supreme court, the present & the ex-presidents; & was on terms of friendship & intimacy with the leading minds of the whole union. She enjoyed the advantage of intimate & confidential intercourse with a class of men of whom ^{not} scarce one now remains — the founders of the republic & their immediate successors. She was in Richmond while the Virginia Legislature was in Session, & then made a long winter journey through North & South Carolina. Thence, she traversed the State of Georgia to Augusta, & from that Capital to Montgomery, Alabama; descending the river afterwards to Mobile. Her route led thence to New Orleans, & up the Mississippi & Ohio to Nashville, Tennessee, on the Cumberland river, & thence into Kentucky to Lexington, averaging a fortnight in each place. After visiting the wonderful Mammoth cave, she descended the Ohio to Cincinnati, the Capital of Ohio State; & again ascending that river, she landed in Virginia, visiting all the natural wonders & beauties of the region. She arrived a second time at New York about the middle of July, 1835. The autumn she spent in the smaller towns of Massachusetts, not neglecting to visit its principal cities, making long visits the whole journey

though in the families of leading men; with excursions to the Mountains of New hampshire & Vermont. All this while the newspapers were her zealous heralds & homagers, so that it might have been a refreshment to her to take up one that did not sing her praises & her progress.

The winter she passed in Boston, always in the houses of persons who had become intimate and dear friends; though of opposite parties sects and aims yet all agreeing in the common feeling of affection for her, in the wish to put her in possession of every means of information or opportunity to become acquainted with the country. Plymouth, the landing-place of the pilgrim fathers in 1620, she visited on occasion of the celebration of "Forefathers' day" Dec 22nd 1835; and the day completed two hundred & fifteen years since the ancestors of the people she had been studying emerged from their little vessel with that independence of mind which eventually dissolved their union with the mother Country, & made of their posterity "a church without a bishop & a state without a king."

Another two months visit in New York, with another month of New England farm-house life, & then came her last American journey — into the West; past Niagara — then by ship across the great inland Seas, & along the prairies beyond the far Lake Shore; — then again through the State of

Ohio, taking the river at Beaver & visiting Rapp's Community Settlement. Thence onward by Pittsburg & the canal route through Pennsylvania, & by rail-road over the Alleghanies; reaching New York in time to sail for England on the 1st of August, 1836.

I have been very careful to give the exact route of the journeys which enabled Harriet Martineau to write her Western life, that, at this distance of time, & with another generation, there might exist no idea that any part of it (as it so the ill ca a) was done in her room — a mere "voyage autour de ma Chambre."

many hearts, as to have become to them like a sister daughter, & next friend & counsellor. The Society of a foreign land is to few travellers more than a stage procession; — to most an enigma: but to her it was a field of action & a host of friends for life. She had entered upon it without any special plan, not even the common one of writing a book. She came for rest & the refreshment of change, & to learn what those principles of Justice & Mercy in the treatment of the least fortunate classes were, which Lord Henly assured her the Americans, whatever their other deficiencies, had succeeded in applying, beyond any other people.

"As to actual knowledge of their country she says, "my mind was nearly a blank". But the best of all knowledge is to know how & what to learn. "I remember" she says again, "that on setting out

for the United States I had a vague idea that there
were thirteen of them, & that was almost the only
idea about them I did possess."

The journal is a full memorandum of facts,
events, statistics & "happenings"; (of which "some persons I
have" to a proverb, "more than others — and she was
one of the persons who have most;) with rapid sketch-
es of personages, & traits of character & scenery; such
jottings of salient points as make the text of the long
running commentary of conversation with friends on
return. It is a journal of thoughts, ideas & queries,
but not of feelings or opinions; though feeling im-
bues the whole.

Her first care is to obtain a thorough knowl-
edge of American politics & parties, theoretically & in their
practical workings, with the whole apparatus of govern-
ments. She watched the office-seekers & the office holders, — with the state of the citizens' minds as shown in
their speech, action, & inaction, — in the motives to which
the newspapers appealed or declined to appeal, — in
sectional & caste prejudices; in the political non-
existence of certain classes. In the course of looking into the economy of the United States, she shared
the life of the solitary pioneers of civilization, & the
life of the fashionable watering places; the varied
modes of existence of the far West, — the plantation &
city life of the South, — the life of the New England
farming populations & fishing villages, — the life of

the statesman, the savant, the jurist, the author, the divine Christian & the philanthropist.

She especially studied the agriculture of the country, with all the land & labour questions it involves, with markets, means of transport and internal improvements. This was the time of Bank & Anti-Bank excitements, Tariff & Anti-tariff, Masonry & Anti-Masonry, temperance & intemperance; and she could study from the life, the Commerce, Manufactures, currency & morals of the country. Slavery, as a part of its economy & intermixed with its morals, — a subject too on which she had so recently written & thought, she could not of course overlook.

But what most deeply interested her was the question, what new type of civilization is to evolve from these new institutions? — and does it already begin to appear? She looked to find what were the points of honour among the people, & what their standard of elegance & politeness: what their ideas about property: what their habits & manners in their homes: what the position of women & the treatment of children: what degree of domestic happiness the result of their Marriages: What the provision for their suffering classes — the criminals, & the deficient or infirm or orphan or in — What the religion of America in its science, spirit & administration was closely observed by her: and so thoroughly was she aware of the importance of the ways in which things are approached, & of the preparation of heart & intellect required, that before setting foot in the country, (on Shipboard in fact) she thought

out the book which was the first she published after leaving it — "How to observe." It gives her methods of coming at facts & getting at the truth through their means.

Her powers of observation were enlarged & strengthened by greater exercise than other persons undergo; for her deafness compelled a more persistent course of enquiry & far more careful & thorough examination than others exercised; so that in conjunction with her conscientious veracity, it was rather a gain than a loss to her as a writer on Manners & Morals. Yet she took the precaution of being always accompanied by a ~~qualified~~ friend; and this made her testimony of double importance. One may be assumed to be mistaken, but in the Mouth of two witnesses, every word is established. Thus obliged by her misfortune to learn at first hand, she soon found by the superior clearness & reliability of her own information how little persons in general know of their own Country. Wherever she went, she set every body to wondering & verifying.— Her habits of mind, both as an Englishwoman & as an individual were more exact than those of Americans in general.

Before coming to the United States, she had written that "Letter to the Deaf," which brought her so near the hearts of all afflicted like herself with the exclusion through failure of the sense of hearing, of which hardly any other than the sufferers from it can know all the sadness.

There is a paper of hers in "Household Words" written of
course long after this time, — "the Deaf Playmate's tale"
which is, in like manner, both heart-rending & cheering in its revelations of suffering & suggestions of the
means of profiting by them. Her frank, self-regu-
lating, unobtrusive method always met its natural re-
ward in placing her on all public occasions, where
she could best hear the Speakers.

I have been thus precise in my statement
that deafness, in her degree & of it was on the
whole a strengthener of her testimony, because slaveholders who never saw her, caught hold of the well
known fact, in order to discredit the value of her
condemnation of their System; just as in Dr.
Johnson's time those who suffered from his judg-
ments affirmed that he was too blind to be believed.

Without a reference to the Map of the United States
and a knowledge of the date, origin & modes of life
of the thirty states she visited, I could not give to Europeans
any sufficient idea of the extent of the opportunities
her genius had opened & her tact felt & seized.
Without a betrayal of confidence I can give but the
slightest idea of the influences she set in motion both
by origination & sympathy. She every where visited
the prisons, the hospitals, the Asylums, the education-
al institutions. The factories, the farms, the plantations
& the Courts of law were equally familiar to her. She
was alternately in the Ball room & the Senate chamber —

the drawing room & the house of assembly. She was the beloved & honoured guest of the wealthiest & the poorest; dwelling by turns in all America could show for palaces, & in the log cabins of the pioneer settlements. She saw the two proscribed races, — the descendants of Africa & the native Indian tribes, in all their various circumstances, & the dominant white race in all its characters. She met men in their families, churches & markets, — their festivals, funerals & weddings, — at land-sales, political gatherings & slave markets.

There are persons of so loving a nature, that without a thought of popularity, they have the gift to make themselves generally & personally beloved; — & she was the chiefest of these. I wish it were allowable for me to name the American families who held her dear as one of their own members, & who spoke of her ever after, & whose descendants speak of her to this hour as one whose remembrance brightens their whole past. My list would be a long one. In some instances there was a tone of regret that she had not always remained where they first knew her. Like doting families who dread to see their youth growing out of youth's peculiar charm into man & womanhood, they wished her always to remain an enquirer within their institutions. They were ready to weep on seeing her quit the pleasant region of Sabbath rest which she found & left them, at this season of her refreshment from toil & preparation for battle. But this feeling of course diminished in exact proportion as her influence made

their mother. and at length, in after years, even Slaveholders seemed to have forgotten their displeasure at her condemnation of American Slavery & to feel as if her philosophy were the only bar between them. Life in their land had been to her a Succession of *Fêtes*. Since Lafayette, the saviour & the guest of the Nations, no one had been received with such distinction the whole land over. They sought her at first as an inspirer & afterwards as a friend & comforter; – and there is an instinct in the public mind to know who can serve it in these particulars. Americans forgot their habitual caution with her. They at first praised & afterwards blamed her like a people who had never heard of such a virtue. Their feelings were in fact more deeply moved by her than She seems to have supposed. They were not subject to the English Conventionalism in the expression of Eulogy & dispraise. The Standard of good breeding in my country was not at that time generally the same on this point. I am not speaking now of that sort of puffing & abuse (it is true) which runs, in all countries alike, to the extent of their sense of policy; but of that uncritical praise to the face, which always disgusted Harriet Martineau as flattery; though in America it simply meant, "you have pleased me: & I will have the satisfaction of telling you so."

But no records of the flatteries of American correspondents remain. Such letters were always burnt. I find, however a letter addressed to the Mother

of Harriet Martineau, from one of the distinguished Southern ~~families~~ ladies with whom she was a guest, Mrs. Gilman, of South Carolina, (which Mrs. ~~Martineau~~ carefully preserved,) as delicate as it ~~was true~~: and I am glad to be able to show exactly how Americans felt towards Harriet Martineau, before they comprehended her highest desires. for such a letter does not express the general feeling.

Letter of Mrs. Gilman.

Charleston S.C.

Dear Madam,

An hour before parting from your daughter, I offered in the fulness of my heart, ~~try~~ & ~~tired~~ to write to you. Knowing the feelings of a mother, I send you this ~~letter~~, as I would give a hungry man a piece of bread: — not because it is the most savory ~~thing~~ in the world, but because a good appetite will make it sweet.

The fortnight Harriet passed with us, (you know she loves that appellation) we shall never forget; not from the development of her fine powers in general society, but from the winning manner in which she gave & inspired confidence at home. I love to remember the frank & hearty air with which, when we had fought through a day of varied & sometimes exhausting engagements, she threw aside her cloak & said to my husband & myself, at 11 O'Clock at night, "Come, now let us have a little talk."

14.

Thus far we looked down into each others'
hearts in those winged midnight hours, & what a
treasure of friendship was garnered up! not for this
world, for alas, we shall probably never meet again, —
but for another, where no wide sea shall separate
us!

I had written thus far when an unusually rapid
scratching of my husband's pen attracted my attention; & peeping over his shoulder, I perceived that he
was writing on the same subject as myself, to
his brother, E. G. Loring, of Boston. It saves me
a little embarrassment to copy his letter, because I
cannot pour out my thoughts as unreservedly to you
on your daughter's merits as I would to another.
    He says: —
    Dear Friend & Brother,
                    I have been for some
days meditating a letter to you on the subject
of Miss Martineau. It was a true & happy impulse
which caused both Caroline & myself to think of send-
ing her a letter of invitation to stay with us as long as
she remained in Charleston. The letter met her in
Richmond, & she has since repeatedly said, gave her great
pleasure. We expected an elegant, gifted, good woman,
but we did not expect, in addition to all this, a lively,
playful, childlike, simplicity-breathing, loving creature,
whose moral qualities as much outshine her intellectual, as these last the ordinary run of mankind. But
exactly so, and without any exaggeration or enthusiasm
in my picture, we found her. On account of the

necessary irregularity & dissipation of her present mode of life, I gave her full liberty to keep her own hours, & to be free from the rules of the family. But No; she found out our hours of family prayer, & always came in most punctually, with her favourite bible, the Portensian edition, which she reads more than any other book. *

In fact though intending to be with us only a fortnight, she at once domesticated & ensconced herself among us, as quietly & closely as if she had come for ten years. Dining out frequently, & passing the evening at one or two parties, as soon as she came home at night & had read at my request a devotional hymn in her own sweet & primitive manner, she would take Caroline on one side & me on the other, & there fixed, eye to eye & soul to soul, would she enchain & enchant us until long after Midnight when we were obliged to tear ourselves away, only out of tenderness to her. I do not think a woman ever lived who had such power to inspire others with affection. So you will say when you know her. So almost every body says who has passed two hours in her society. One peculiar bond of interest between us was, that all her early attempts at publication which laid the foundation of her subsequent fame, were issued in the "Monthly Repository," just about the time when I used to, prepare for that periodical a series of papers called, "the critical Synopsis of the Monthly Repository," consisting of remarks on every piece

* This "Portensian Bible" was the gift of Mr Worthington, her betrothed, the last time they met.

inserted in that work. We passed several hours in looking over these volumes. She never knew the author or his name, but told me she used to figure him as a fat old gentleman in New England, sitting in his easy-chair, with a blue coat & yellow buttons, pronouncing decisions on her youthful compositions. On the second of the two Sundays she passed with us I taught her a part of John's first chapter, in Greek. Her accuracy, & determination to pass over not a single principle in grammar or criticism, however minute, was astonishing. She has a wonderful power of inspiring confidence, & extracting from those she is interested in, the whole history of their past lives. This power was exercised over several of our leading politicians at Washington & elsewhere, as well as over us. Mr. Calhoun took infinite pains to indoctrinate her in the system of Nullification. When we dined with General H——, we were invited an hour before the other guests, that he might give her, at her request, his views on Slavery. She studiously avoided arguing on these subjects, but quietly & keenly directed her attention & questions to gentlemen of all parties, in such a manner as to bring out the whole scope & detail of their several opinions. She made no secret of her aversion to Slavery. She perceives & acknowledges, however, that the movements of the abolitionists have injured & retarded the cause of Slaves here. Many little presents were sent her & Miss Jeffrey while here, & this mode of attention would probably have been manifested much more frequently had she remained longer. Mrs—'s gift (your Louisa will be interested in it,) was six linen-cambric handkerchiefs marked with various emblems of Harriet's character & fame.

She threw out many little pleasantries on the
six carriages that were offered daily, for her use, (one
of which stood regularly at our door at 11 O'clock daily)
threatening to make a provision of them & sit in the
first. We gave her no party on account of our accumulated
engagements, but invited friends to breakfast with her
She loves children, & children love her. She has brought
ours a Bible-play, for Sunday evenings, in which adults
join with great interest. On the last day of her being
in Charleston she resisted several invitations in order to
comply with our girls' desire to have her visit their dancing
school.

Caroline & I accompanied her eighteen miles out
of town, where we spent the day rambling in the woods
or reading her works. We could not have done any thing
else. On our return home at night, we found that our
Louisa, (fourteen years old) had beguiled the time by composing
her first piece of music, called the "Martineau Cotillion." I
have purchased the Boston edition of her Illustrations, for
my wife, & Miss Martineau has written, after a little coax-
ing from her, one or more sentences in every number,
giving a previous list of history, or remark respecting
the tales. She could hear most of my sermons through
her horn, & has, I trust, benefited me by her remarks &
encouragements. She is a deep adept in the philosophy of
Carlyle, the reviewer of Burns, and the "Characteristics,"
in the Edinburgh. She devoted several reading hours to
these articles, for us & Colonel C's family, our charming neigh-

down. She will speak of Coleridge & Wordsworth, & Barrett Smith, to your heart's content.
neighbors. Colonel P., the Senator from Columbia,
who says to her in a recent letter,— "how can you make
people love you so,"— has purchased her portrait by
Osgood. General H— sent her a set of the Southern
Review, & we had a delicious evening after she went away,
marking the authors' names, & talking her over with
the——s. She continued to run through several books during our fortnight, & answers writing to her numerous correspondents & bringing up her journal; yet she was never in a hurry,— never kept people waiting; & seemed
only to hanker for long sweet private conversations
with Caroline & myself. Her friend Miss Jeffery is
an original, keen, frank, intelligent young lady, & secures
friends in every quarter. My wife abandoned herself to
the pleasure of intercourse with them. Her deportment
to them was of resistless hilarity, while mine was more
solemn under the painful consciousness that our intercourse
must soon be over. My letter is a poor, faint idea
of what you will find her. Her laugh is exquisite-
ly amicable, frequent & joyous. My wife is going
to write to Harriet's Mother. She adores her brother
James, a young Liverpool minister, more than
any body else in the world,[+] & next to him stands
Mr. Furness. But E. G. Loring will step in between her
brother James & Mr. Furness." — — —

My long sojourn, dear Madam, will give you

[+] Note by Mrs. Gilman "Except her Mother".

a correct impression of the intercourse with your daughter on our part. I will only add that her journey through the United States has been thus far one of triumphs; — the best kind of triumph too, for she has been borne along on our hearts. —

Remember us to "brother James & sister Ellen," & other members of a family whom "not having seen we love."

Yours respectfully,
Caroline Gilman

And so felt the the Madisons, the Clays, the Channings, the Bowditches, and all the long list of those who felt themselves honored in receiving such a guest. Her visit to the Madisons was never to be forgotten by them or herself. All parties possessed that great social gift — the power of talking & letting talk. Each day of her visit to these eminent personages, the whole time from morning to night was spent in rapid conversation. Mr. Madison's share was on the principles & history of the Constitution of the United States: and his insight into the contemporaneous condition of other nations & his his personal survey of the affairs of that period, with his abundant household anecdotes of Washington, Franklin, Jefferson & their contemporaries, gave her almost a reproduction of those times.

Chief Justice Marshall was no less charmed by such intercourse than the Madison family. He even gave her a circular letter of moral credit (so to

call it) in every inhabitant of the Country, which
had she been before unknown would have secured for
her every attention & accommodation. There was something
in the minds of these elders of the republic, minds of
original greatness formed by a real life of political toil
in the midst of tempests, – which was in harmony
with her own. She was but just in time for the
good fortune of thus coming into the line of our American
traditions; for all these great men died shortly after.

Her visit to Jefferson's university at Charlottesville. Virginia, made the delight of the professors & their families.
She was the only English traveller who had ever penetrated
to their studious retreat. At Cambridge, ~~she was received~~
~~among the most distinguished families~~ among the most distinguished families
she sat by the fountain-head of the literary life of the
Union.

The venerable Albert Gallatin was greatly attracted by her. He could appreciate the accuracy of her
various knowledge, & it was a labour of love to him
to try to add to it. At once shrewd & chivalrous, pen-
etrating & benevolent, he could not but leave his impress
distinctly on her memory. I quote from her journal:–
"

First Interview with Mr Gallatin.

Sept 24th. Mr Gallatin called. Old man. Began career in 1787. Been three times in England. Twice as Minister. Found George the Fourth a cypher. Louis Philippe very different. Will manage all himself, & keep what he has. William the Fourth silly, as Duke of Clarence. Gallatin would have the President a cypher too, if he could: — i.e. would have him annual, so that all would be done by the Ministry. As this cannot get be, he prefers a four years term, without renewal, to the present plan, or to six years. The office was made for the man — Washington, who was wanted (as well as fit) to reconcile all parties. Bad office: but well filled till now. Too much power for one man; — therefore too high a stake; — therefore it fills all men's thoughts to the detriment of better things. Jackson a "pugnacious animal." This the reason, (in the absence of interested motives) of his present bad conduct.

New Englanders the best people perhaps in the world, — prejudiced, but able, honest & homogeneous. Compounds elsewhere. In Pennsylvania the German settlers the most ignorant, but best political economists. Give any price for best land, & hold it all. Compound in New York. Emigrants a sad drawback. Slaves & gentry in the South. In Gallatin's recollection, Ohio, Illinois (?) & Indiana had not a white except a French station or two: now, a million & a half (?) of flourishing whites. Maize the cause of rapid accumulation. Makes a white a capitalist between February & November; while the Indian remains in statu quo, & when

22.

[the next page begins
with 1. she writes to her mother.

accumulation once begins — &c. &c. Gov't cant resume
land. People are gov't — & will have all the lands. [Pon-
der this.] He drew up a plan of selling lands. Would have
sold at $ 2. Was soon brought down to $ 1¼, with credit. Then,
as it is bad for subjects to be debtors to a Democratic Government
reduction supplied the place of credit, & the price was brought
down to ¼ dol.

All great changes have been effected by the Democratic
party from the first, up to the Universal Suffrage which prac-
tically exists. Aristocracy must arise (?) Traders rise, some
few fall: but most retain, with pains, their elevation. — Bad
trait here, — fraudulent bankruptcies, tho' dealing is generally
fair. Reason, — that enterprise must be encouraged; must
exist to such a degree as to be liable to be carried too far.

Would have no U.S. Bank. Would have free Banking as
Soon as practicable. Cant be got. Thinks Jackson all wrong
about the Bank: but has changed his opinion as to its powers. It has no political power, but prodigious Commercial.
[Is not this political in this Country?] If the Bank be not
necessary, better avoid allowing this power. — Banks had
not overpapered the Country.

Gallatin is tall, bald, toothless, speaks with a burr,
looks venerable & courteous: opened out & apologized
for his full communication. — Kissed my hand.

~~Van Buren is the chief of the Tories.~~

Sept. 25. Clay is the father of the Tariff system. A hearty Or-
ator. Is it the Irish & Low Labourers who riot
against Abolition? Fine, it was so like a brutality

— "... General Mason, of Virginia, with his wife and daughters are loading us with attentions. He is one of the most finished gentlemen I ever saw, & if I am not mistaken, one of the most sensible of men. He insists on our whole party, to Niagara taking possession of his country house on Lake Erie, which he writes to direct his son to prepare for us. His son is Governor, at Detroit —

Now shall I ever tell you what we are doing! In the first place, half our day is taken up with visitors. Such trains! — The late Mayor, to bid me welcome, — lawyers & candidates for office, interested in poor laws & what not. Some of my honours are, having three special orders issued for my things to pass the custom house untouched; — tributes from Authors, — a letter from the principal booksellers of the State requesting leave to reciprocate for any work I may think of publishing, & begging me to designate from their book-list, what works they shall have the pleasure to present me with. ~~~~~~~~~~~~~~~ So far among the New Yorkers. ~~~~~~~~~~~ the impression I made ~~~~~~~~~ among the Pennsylvanians & ~~~~~ the New Englanders. ~~~~~~~ Now was her first meeting with those she always called her American brother & sister, Mr. & Mrs Furness. It was, after service, at Church. "He came straight down to us from the pulpit & begged me to accept the hospitality of his house first when I go to Philadelphia. He was almost in tears & so near me, it was so like a brotherly

meeting. He & all the Unitarian Ministers in New York have called. —The dinner party yesterday was quite perfect. pleasant company. All from the South & therefore well behaved. Most of the company said they should call on us at Washington or Charleston. On Thursday morning we start, — first to Patterson, N. Jer. will way, to see the falls of the Passaic, then up the Hudson to West Point where we spend a whole day, then to Dr. Hosack's at Hyde Park for a day or two. On to Tivoli for two or three days, & then to Troy, to stay with Mrs. Warren, & see the beautiful neighbourhood. She will take us to see Miss Sedgwick, at Stockbridge. Then to the Falls of Niagara, stopping at the prettiest places by the way. I am told that the violence about the Slavery question [of which she had heard before landing] is all among the Irish & low labourers, who are afraid of the colored people being raised to an equality with them. If this is true, it alters the state of the case.

"Mr Van Buren had let them know at Auburn that I was going, & had commissioned a friend of his to see that I saw every thing. So Colonel Lewis, the Superintendent of the prison was ready to do what he never does, — go round the prison with us — among the convicts. I am not going to send you a critique on this prison. — I have not decided what to think of it further than this, — that however good the system may be here, it would not do with us. Hundreds would be committing grand larceny to get in. Tomorrow, at dawn, we rise to walk by lake Erie! & at 9 we set out for Niagara! — "Sure its no me". We now, on the shores of Erie, & as

easily as I could get to Stockwell! We really feel no
fatigue or trouble. Nothing can exceed the civility we
have met with every where, & we feel that there is a sim-
plicity of manner betokening a moral purity, which cannot
but banish all fear. Do not think me run away with
by the enjoyment of my journey. Remember that I
say nothing yet, because I know nothing of the religious
& intellectual state of society; but we are more & more
surprised every day at nothing having been said of the
engaging & cheering ingenuousness of manners, which
is the charm of the country to us. Your birth-day has
not been forgotten, dearest Mother, nor ever will be
while I am on earth & not under it. We find no letters
here, & must wait till we get to Philadelphia, where I am
sure some will await us. My Mother's last, is enough to live
upon for a long time. I shall go on, writing home, — I cannot
help it. I feel all my powers unanealed, & begin to fancy I
may do great things after this glorious journey. Give
me your sympathy on this eve of that great day of
my life, — the day which is to disclose Niagara to me.
I have been obliged to give up General Wadsworth for
the present, but hope to go by & bye.

Oct. 14th.
Niagara

You must not expect a description from
me. One might as well give an idea of the Kingdom
of Heaven by images of Jasper & Topazes, as of what
we have been seeing, by writing of hues & dimensions.
Except the Hurricane at sea, it is the only sight I ever
saw that I had utterly failed to imagine. It is not so gran-

dear that strikes me so much, but its unimaginable beauty.
All images of softness fail before it — Think of a double
rainbow issuing from a rock a hundred feet below, & almost
completing its circle by nearly lighting on one's head.
The slowness with which the waters roll over is most majes-
tic. There is none of the hurry & trouble of common water-
falls; but the green transparent mass seems to ooze
over the edges. The ascent of the spray, seen some miles
off, surprised me: it did not hang like a cloud, but curled
vigorously up, like smoke from a cannon, or a new fire.
We have crossed the ferry, & done more than in my
present state of intoxication, I can well remember or tell
you of. On the spot, I feel quite sane, — sure footed &
reasonable; but when I sat down to dinner, I
found what the excitement had been. I could
not tell boiled from roast Beef! — & my only resource
was to go out again as soon as we could leave the
table. & now, I am very sleepy. I suspected I should
be disappointed, & told Miss Sedgwick so. She was right in
saying that it was impossible. If one looks mere-
ly for a Cataract, it would be easy to say, "dear me! I
could fancy a rock twice as high as that, & a river
twice as broad." But I do not think my imagination
could conceive of such colouring; & I was wholly un-
prepared for the beauty of the surrounding scenery. Frag-
ments of Rainbows start up, & flit & vanish, like phantoms
at a signal from the sun. We have watched the growth
of the Moon — "the Niagara Moon"; — & there she is, at
last.

Turn over & print from back of page 4

at her very brightest, bless her! — What pleasure there is in a wholly new idea! It never occurred to me before that there can never be a cloudless sky at Niagara. A light fleecy rack is always over the falls & the watcher may here see the process of cloud-making. No more now. Rejoice with me that I have now seen the best that my eyes can behold in this life *

I wish I could bring all the enemies in this world here. They must cease to hate as surely as they would in Heaven."

* I find among her papers the Guide's certificate to a feat she does not mention — that she penetrated behind the sheet of water to the extreme wall at the end of the horse shoe hollow. Years after Colonel Devens of Norwich told these on his return from an American tour that the Guide, pointing it out to him said — "We call that Harriet Martineau's Rock."

Dearest Mother, We are as well & happy as possible. Our friends have been busy in our service during our little absence. Mr. King had prepared a letter of credit on all the banks in the States, so that my money matters will be easily arranged every where; — the Fergusons had laid plans about forwarding our letters; And General Mason had prepared a handful of letters for us for almost every place on our route, & has written to the governor of ~~Philadel~~ ~~to have this~~ empty house ready for our whole party. Mrs. Mason said that if we would visit them again next summer the family will all go with us, the tour of the Western lakes! The General brought the Secretary of War, Mr. Dickinson, to make his compliments & hope to meet us at Washington in the Winter. So many letters had been sent that half the company at the hotel were ready to welcome us. Washington Irving was one, & we had a few ~~minutes~~ talk with him at the landing place. He was engaged to dine on the opposite shore, but sent an accomplished escort to us in Mr. Morris, the Editor of the New York Mirror. Meeting Mr. Morris he cried out, "I've seen her! — so may you. Fly ~~right~~ away up the hill!" O, West point! Whatever I may see, this will abide, as my first vision. The greenest of all green terraces high raised above the brimming river, — Mountains piled all round, — the ruins of Fort Putnam on the steep, the distant town of Newburgh ~~seen~~ between the hills, the elegant sloops tacking & gliding below, the scarlet maple & red Beech beginning to variegate the woods, the most golden of sunlights bathing the whole, — this was almost too much at noon: but when the Cadets were at the evening parade, the french horns echoing from the terrace & the evening gun ~~hooting~~ among the Mountains, it was almost too much to be borne. — — In the

afternoon we climbed to Fort Putnam, & saw the cell
where poor André is said to have been confined. Next
Morning, I stole out alone, to Kosciusko's Garden, a
little rocky retreat shut in from all but the
river, where is the patriot's turf seat, and a stone fountain.
The only alteration since his time is his name being carved
on the fountain. One of the cadets was lying musing on
a high point of rock, & another accosted me with the utmost
politeness to tell me some anecdotes of the place. These young
men are considered the flower of the States; & indeed, I never
saw finer manners. We had a very long talk about their
academy, American politics &c, & I learned much from them.
We are struck above all things with what I have heard
nobody observe, viz: the ingenuous, open, innocence of
manner of the gentlemen here. It is too soon to speak
with certainty; but there is a respect in their treatment of others
which I never saw equalled except in individual instances. We
have seen none that we could for a moment fancy profligate;
and the freedom of social intercourse between the young people
is very great. The young folks in a family take the lead, or at
least, please themselves in all things as they grow up; and
the parents seem to feel it a proper relief that their children
act for themselves as soon as they become capable. I con-
clude this is what Dr. Channing means by "filial in-
subordination": a term which can only apply where parents wish to preserve their authority; which is not the case
often, here. This is what we have observed & been told;
and it is confirmed by the wonder of our friends in this
house at "Pride & Prejudice." They cannot understand
the book: & ask us whether in England, a foolish moth-

www.ingramcontent.com/pod-product-compliance
Lightning Source LLC
Chambersburg PA
CBHW030900260626
47169CB00008B/2616